Still-Life Stew

Helena Clare Pittman

Illustrated by Victoria Raymond

Hyperion Books for Children

New York

Printed in Singapore

First Edition
1 3 5 7 9 10 8 6 4 2

The illustrations for this book are constructed from many separate elements, each
of which is first sculpted from a colored modeling compound called Sculpey III
and then baked in an oven until hard. Once each component of the piece is com-
plete, the artist paints them with acrylic paints and then—using glue, armature
wire, and even toothpicks—assembles the pieces into what the reader sees.

This book is set in 18-point Cochin.
Designed by Stephanie Bart-Horvath.
Photography by Monica Stevenson.

Library of Congress Cataloging-in-Publication Data

Pittman, Helena Clare.
Still-life stew / Helena Clare Pittman; illustrated by Victoria Raymond.—1st ed.
p.   cm.
Summary: Rosa grows a variety of bright and beautiful vegetables, picks them,
paints a picture, and then makes them into a tasty stew.
ISBN 0-7868-0251-0 (trade)—ISBN 0-7868-2206-6 (lib. bdg.)
[1. Vegetables—Fiction. 2. Painting—Fiction.] I. Raymond, Victoria, ill. II. Title.
PZ7.P689St   1998
[E]—dc21   97-25646

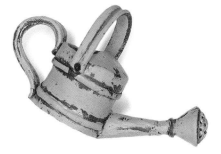

This is **Rosa's garden**, growing things fo

osa's painting. **Rosa's still-life painting**.

Rosa's paper is big and empty.
Flapping, empty,
big and shining in the sun.

Rosa picks **tomatoes**.
Heart-shaped, plum-shaped, clouds-in-a-stormy-sky-shaped.
Bright red, light red. Yellow-orange, greeny-red.

She picks **peppers**.
Lopsided, flute-sided, slippy, slopey,
up-and-down-sided.
Twisty, curling, coiled and spiraling.
Yellow-sweet, red-hot, and green
crunchy peppers.

Eggplants, fat and glossy.
Seedy, meaty, dark black-purple,
white and pink.

"And something more!"
says Rosa.

Wide **zucchini**. Long zucchini.
Loopy, curvy, striped zucchini.
Rubbery, scratchy, oversize, and teeny-weeny.

Long, lanky **leeks** squeak as Rosa picks them.
Sleek, sandy leeks, even when you wash them.
Lovely, lively, leaning, light green leeks.

"And more!"
says Rosa.

Carrots gangly, long and triangly.
Straggly, spidery, bushy-greened.
Pointy, bendy, fat, and skinny.

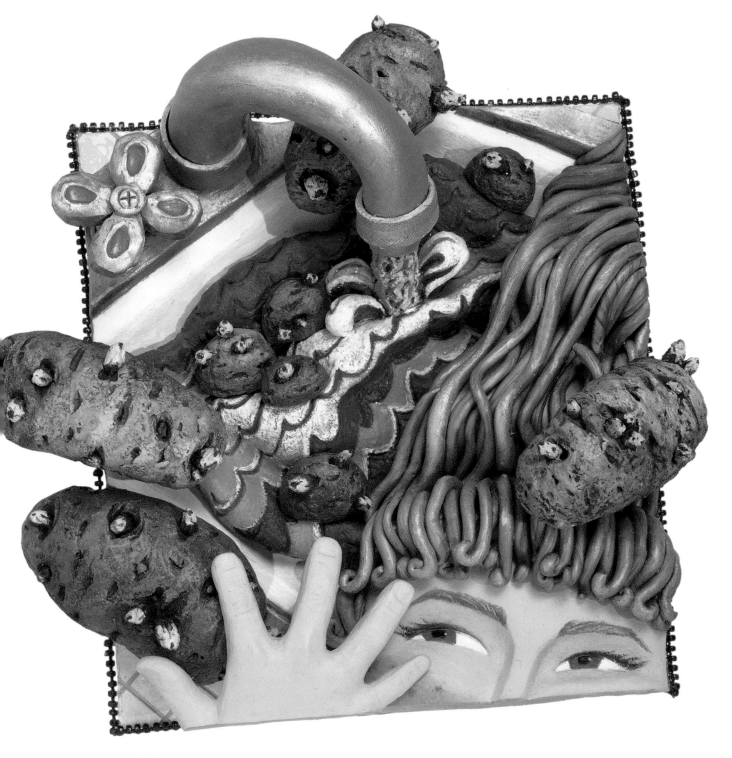

Potatoes. Lumpy-tumbly, wobbly potatoes.
Runaway, gawking-with-eyes potatoes.
Brown, bobbing-in-the-sink potatoes.
Squeaky-when-you-scrub-them-clean potatoes.

Rosa's white paper is bright
against the sky.
Rosa's white paper is snapping
in the breeze.

Rosa's white paper is big enough for . . .

"More!" says Rosa.
Garlic. Pungent, shiny, sticky, garlicky garlic.
Smelling-all-day-long garlic.

Deep, dark **spinach**. Green, gritty, earthy spinach. Stalky, stringy, rooty spinach.

Bean-greeny **green beans.**
Snapping-wet, stuffed with eeny-beanies.
Bulgy, bumpy, sweet-green string beans.

Rosa picks and digs until she has . . .

"Enough!"

Enough to fill her **flapping, empty**

big, white, waiting paper.

"Now," says Rosa, setting up her rainbow paints.

She dabs bright orange streaks.
She brushes red, blotched and blotty, tomatoey-splotty.

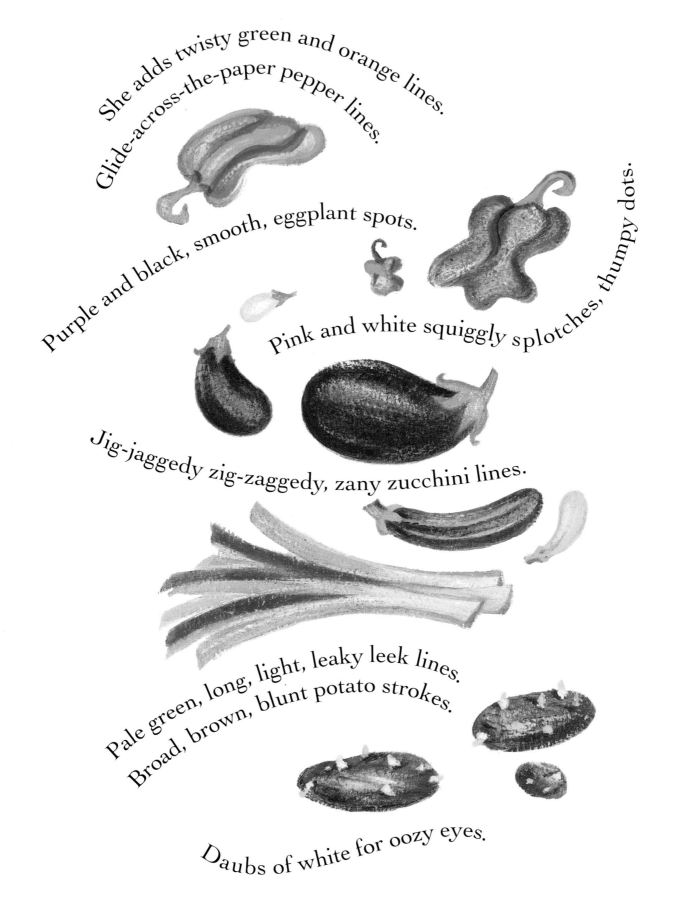

She adds twisty green and orange lines.

Glide-across-the-paper pepper lines.

Purple and black, smooth, eggplant spots.

Pink and white squiggly splotches, thumpy dots.

Jig-jaggedy zig-zaggedy, zany zucchini lines.

Pale green, long, light, leaky leek lines.

Broad, brown, blunt potato strokes.

Daubs of white for oozy eyes.

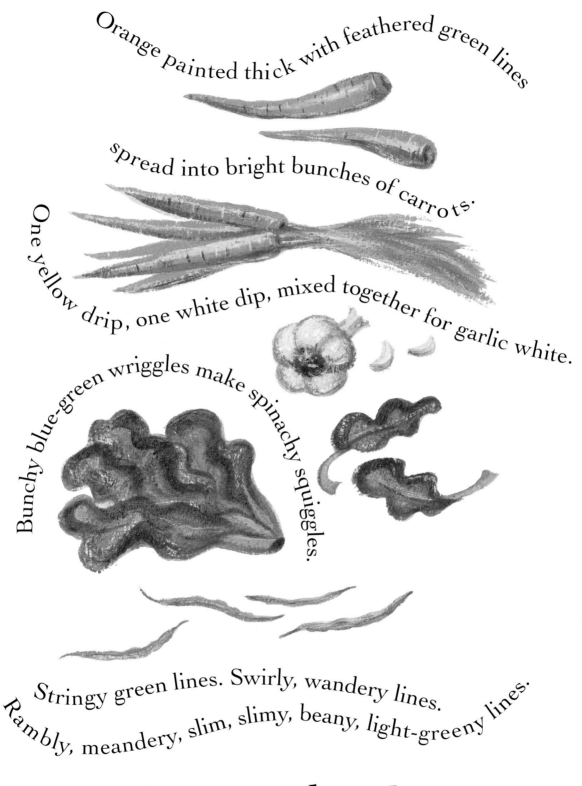

Orange painted thick with feathered green lines

spread into bright bunches of carrots.

One yellow drip, one white dip, mixed together for garlic white.

Bunchy blue-green wriggles make spinachy squiggles.

Stringy green lines. Swirly, wandery lines. Rambly, meandery, slim, slimy, beany, light-greeny lines.

"There!" says Rosa.

Rosa's bold, bright, curvy,
colorful still-life picture is finished.

"And one thing more!" says Rosa.

Cut, dice, chop, and slice.
Crush, cube, quarter, and snap.
Salt, pepper, simmer, and serve.

Rosa's chewy, chompy, tasty, slurpy, yummy,
still-life stew is ready to eat.

"M-mmm-m," says Rosa.

The Story Behind th

Photo: Susan Gaber

Recipe for One Fun Book

1 idea	1 writer
1 tablespoon of fun	1 artist
1 cupful of excitement	2 imaginations
An assortment of words	

- Start with author, who is also an art teacher.
- Enter inspiration, in the form of beautiful, colorful vegetables: eggplants, zucchini, peppers, tomatoes, onions.
- Have art students draw beautiful still-life pictures of vegetables. Hang pictures all over walls.
- Bring vegetables home to make a stew.
- Book idea is born: *Still-Life Stew*!
- Author writes manuscript, and then artist adds her special ingredients.

Making of Still-Life Stew

Photo: Merlin vanGelderen

Ingredients
for Making Pictures

1 artist	Piles of fresh vegetables
1 story	Heaps of sticky colored clay
1 pair of hands and eyes	Lots of glue and wire
1 oven	Boxes and boxes of toothpicks
1 dream	Bright tubes of shiny paint
Tons of creativity and	Fat and skinny brushes
boundless energy	Soap and water to clean

- Preheat oven to 300°F.
- Roll the clay. Pound, curve, and shape.
- Place clay pieces in the oven. Bake anywhere from ten minutes to one hour.
- Take art out and let it cool.
- Arrange pieces to make a picture. Press and glue together. Toothpicks and wire connect clay pieces and hold them in place.
- Time to set up your palette. Brush on the paints thick and bright until the picture looks just right!

Rosa's Still-Life Stew

6 potatoes, cubed	15 mushrooms, halved
8 tomatoes, quartered	2 bunches of spinach,
6 leeks, chopped	roots and stalks trimmed
3 peppers, seeded and sliced	6 cloves of garlic, crushed
2 eggplants, diced	1 tablespoon of olive oil
5 zucchini, sliced thick	Salt, pepper, and spices to taste
29 string beans, snapped	2 cups of water

Brown mushrooms, leeks, garlic, peppers, and zucchini in oil. Add other ingredients and sauté for 10 minutes. Then add water, salt, pepper, and spices. Simmer slowly in a big pot for $1\frac{1}{2}$ hours. Serves 4–6.